Benefits of Turning 30

A Comprehensive Analysis

Wilbert Wellington-Boot

Chief Editor Tony Tanner

Wellington Boot Publishing

ISBN:
978-1-9993336-0-7

DEDICATION

This book is dedicated to my Grandmother, who untimely passed just before my 30th Birthday. We will never forgive ourselves for oversleeping the morning of your memorial service. I hope Grandad and I have a chance to make it up to you in Heaven one day. Rest well.

CONTENTS

‘Life is islands of ecstasy in an ocean of ennui, and after the age of thirty land is seldom seen.’

- Luke Rhinehart

CHAPTER 1

Interest in Nights Out Beyond Midnight

CHAPTER 2

Hangover Recovery Period

CHAPTER 3

Speed of Weight Gain

CHAPTER 4

Overall Physical Appearance

CHAPTER 5

Ability to Stay Fit

CHAPTER 6

Career Motivation & Flexibility

CHAPTER 7

Number, Cost & Regularity of Weddings

CHAPTER 8

Number of Baby Announcements

Number of Baby Announcements

Number of Baby Announcements

CHAPTER 9

Enthusiasm for Dating

CHAPTER 10

Overall Outlook on Life

THE END

ABOUT THE AUTHOR

In Wilbert's early 20's, the world was still healing from the Vietnam War, which Wilbert refers to as the generation of 'freeloaders, hippies and sexual disease'… also known as the 1960s.

Wilbert was a newly divorced young man and filled with regret at that time. He was determined to find his vocation in life and discover the man he wanted to become.

This period in Wilbert's life also coincided with a boom in nightlife entertainment across New York and London. Newly liberated, Wilbert became enamoured with the clubbing scene, even using a portion of his trust to become a part owner of several clubs. He often fondly reminisces of the closing party at Club 54 where Diana Ross graced the audience with a performance.

Living a life fuelled by drugs, alcohol and pursuits of the flesh left Wilbert unsatisfied and yearning for substance. As growing global tensions again rose due to the escalating Cold War, Wilbert craved stability in his life and once again exchanged vows. This marriage was short-lived and at 29, Wilbert found himself divorced.

Wilbert's grandfather, William, became concerned that his grandson would relapse into his old life of debauchery. He offered Wilbert a contingency deal - One last blow out at Wilbert's favourite club, Copacabana. In exchange, he asked for a promise that he would once and for all part with his youthful ways. Aside from some light cocaine use, Wilbert kept his word to his Grandfather and began a decade of complacency and normality.

THE **BENEFITS** OF SERIES

From politics and marriage, to childbirth and divorce, The *Benefits Of* series represents the life-time work of celebrated author Wilbert Wellington-Boot, whose unrivalled and encyclopaedic collection of studies has been published for generation after generation to enjoy.

For more comprehensive analysis of other topics, look no further than a *Benefits Of* book today.

www.wilbertwellingtonboot.com

Printed in Poland
by Amazon Fulfillment
Poland Sp. z o.o., Wrocław